Dear Parents:

Congratulations! Your child is taking the first steps on an exciting journey. The destination? Independent reading!

D0059264

STEP INTO READING® will help your child get there. The program offers five steps to reading success. Each step includes fun stories and colorful art or photographs. In addition to original fiction and books with favorite characters, there are Step into Reading Non-Fiction Readers, Phonics Readers and Boxed Sets, Sticker Readers, and Comic Readers—a complete literacy program with something to interest every child.

Learning to Read, Step by Step!

Ready to Read   Preschool–Kindergarten
• big type and easy words • rhyme and rhythm • picture clues
For children who know the alphabet and are eager to begin reading.

Reading with Help   Preschool–Grade 1
• basic vocabulary • short sentences • simple stories
For children who recognize familiar words and sound out new words with help.

Reading on Your Own   Grades 1–3
• engaging characters • easy-to-follow plots • popular topics
For children who are ready to read on their own.

Reading Paragraphs   Grades 2–3
• challenging vocabulary • short paragraphs • exciting stories
For newly independent readers who read simple sentences with confidence.

Ready for Chapters   Grades 2–4
• chapters • longer paragraphs • full-color art
For children who want to take the plunge into chapter books but still like colorful pictures.

STEP INTO READING® is designed to give every child a successful reading experience. The grade levels are only guides; children will progress through the steps at their own speed, developing confidence in their reading. The F&P Text Level on the back cover serves as another tool to help you choose the right book for your child.

CALGARY PUBLIC LIBRARY

Remember, a lifetime love of reading starts with a single step!

JUL   2019

For my children,
Ruby, Lucas, and Theo Weinberg,
and our friend Jonah Crowgey
—J.L.

Text copyright © 2018 by Penguin Random House LLC
Cover art and interior illustrations copyright © 2018 by Mike Yamada

All rights reserved. Published in the United States by Random House Children's Books,
a division of Penguin Random House LLC, New York.

Step into Reading, Random House, and the Random House colophon are registered trademarks
of Penguin Random House LLC.

Visit us on the Web!
StepIntoReading.com
rhcbooks.com

Educators and librarians, for a variety of teaching tools, visit us at RHTeachersLibrarians.com

Library of Congress Cataloging-in-Publication Data is available upon request.

ISBN 978-0-399-55461-2 (trade) — ISBN 978-0-399-55462-9 (lib. bdg.) —
ISBN 978-0-399-55463-6 (ebook)

Printed in the United States of America
10 9 8 7 6 5 4 3 2

This book has been officially leveled by using the F&P Text Level Gradient™ Leveling System.

Random House Children's Books supports the First Amendment and celebrates the right to read.

GO, GO, CARS!

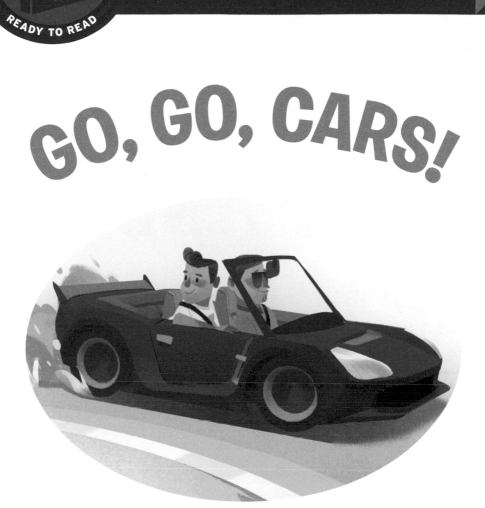

by Jennifer Liberts
illustrated by Mike Yamada

Random House 🏠 New York

Toy car.

Race car.

Time to play.

Small car.

Big car.

Drive away!

Green light.

Fast cars.

Yellow light—
slow.

Red light.

Stop!

Now go, go, go!

Beep, beep!
Old car.

New car.

Vroom!

Shiny sports car—
zoom, zoom, zoom!

Cars that purr.

Cars that roar.

Cars that have
too many doors!

Cars need oil.

Cars need gas.

Cars need great big bubble baths!

WASH

Dry the car.

Now hit the road!

We love cars.

Go, cars, go!